Baron Stow

Little Mary

An Illustration of the Power of Jesus to Save even the Youngest

Baron Stow

Little Mary
An Illustration of the Power of Jesus to Save even the Youngest

ISBN/EAN: 9783337056582

Printed in Europe, USA, Canada, Australia, Japan

Cover: Foto ©Andreas Hilbeck / pixelio.de

More available books at **www.hansebooks.com**

LITTLE MARY,

AN ILLUSTRATION

OF

THE POWER OF JESUS

TO

SAVE EVEN THE YOUNGEST.

With an Introduction

BY BARON STOW, D.D.

BOSTON:

GOULD AND LINCOLN,

59 WASHINGTON STREET.

1861.

Electrotyped and Printed by
W. F. DRAPER, ANDOVER, MASSACHUSETTS.

Introduction.

—∞≫⊙≪∞—

NEAR the close of last autumn, the newspapers contained the following brief notice:

DIED, at Concord, N. H., November 6, of organic disease of the heart, MARY ACHSAH, YOUNGEST DAUGHTER OF JOSEPH A. AND ANN W. GILMORE, *aged thirteen.*

In thousands of cases, every one interesting to the small circle of the bereaved, such a record is the last that meets the public eye; except, it may be, a few commemorative words cut in the headstone that marks the resting-place of the youthful sleeper.

The loved and loving one, whose early departure from this earth-life was thus summarily chronicled, may never have imagined that she was distinguished, either by nature or by grace, for anything worthy of a special memorial, or deemed that any of her utterances or acts would be collected and embalmed for fadeless preservation. But those who knew her well, and especially some who were often near her during her last months of bodily suffering and spiritual triumph, expressed a strong conviction that a faithful narrative of her religious experience might be useful as an illustration of the power of Christ to save the young. The family group had all the incidents, and many more than could be transferred to paper, deeply engraven in their heart of hearts, and needed not, for their own sakes, another record; but a large circle of relatives and friends were anxious to possess a fuller account than could be gathered from oral communications. These demands it was thought best to supply; and the work, confessedly one of much delicacy, was intrusted to the individual who could do it the greatest justice, — Mary's eldest brother, a member of the Senior Class in the Newton Theological Institution. To him it would be — to him it has been — a "*labor of love.*"

I have read in manuscript the entire narrative, and regard it as prepared with commendable judiciousness and fidelity. I discover nothing overdrawn, nothing colored for the sake of effect. My acquaintance with the amiable Mary was familiar from her infancy, and she had the place of a good child in my affection. During the earlier stages of her illness, while she was at the Franconia Mountains, I frequently saw her, and was tenderly interested in her religious exercises. Her little heart impatiently beating against its walls was a fit emblem of her emotional nature struggling to throw off a burden of whose character she had an indefinite conception, but of which she was painfully conscious. I saw her also when hope of her recovery had well-nigh vanished, and heard from her thin, bloodless lips the breathings of a soul " willing rather to be absent from the body and present with the Lord." She was all that the hand of fraternal love has described, and the readers of this touching story may accept the whole as a just picture of the dear one —

" Not lost, but gone before."

The author says, in a statement now before me, " I have tried to adapt it to the capacity of children, ... that thus both parents and children might read and understand it; but I feel that the sudden maturity of little Mary's Christian experience was such that one or two of the chapters must be incomprehensible to any one who has not 'the mind of the Spirit.'" And he declares himself willing to sacrifice the graces of mere style "to the one object of presenting a *truthful* sketch of what the Lord Jesus did for a child of thirteen summers." The reader will find the sketch indeed truthful, and the style like female loveliness —

"When unadorned, adorned the most."

Soon after Mary's decease, her pastor, for whom she had great respect, — the Rev. Dr. Flanders, — preached a discourse, in which he gave his own impressions respecting her case, as a disciple of Christ. He is well known as a careful observer of all the forms of Christian development, and as eminently reliable in his discriminations and judgments. To a sympathizing congregation he said:

"The scenes of her last illness and her departing hours were so marked with peaceful trust in Christ, that I have felt it my *duty* to give you a somewhat full account of them. In recounting the last hours of one's experience on earth it becomes the Christian minister to guard against a more hopeful presentation than the facts warrant, lest, in his desire to soothe the wounded sensibilities of the bereaved, he may inflict lasting injury on others. It would be better to withhold all reference to the hopeful dead, than that by any over-wrought statement harm should be done to the souls of the living. But the case before us needs no coloring. The scene *as it was* is sufficiently beautiful and impressive. I am grateful to God that in my ministry, among my dear people, I have been permitted to witness such a scene in the last illness of one so young, and have the opportunity to describe it."

On the 9th of November, at mid-day, we stood amid the quiet shades of Mount Auburn, and worshipped Him who is "the Resurrection and the Life." There was the casket enclosing all that was mortal of little Mary.

"Like blossomed tree o'erturned by vernal storm,
   Lovely in death the beauteous ruin lay."

There was the opened grave ready to receive this new treasure to its trust. The ground was carpeted with fallen foliage imbrowned by autumnal frosts. The sun shone genially through the leafless trees. It was an hour of solemn, impressive beauty. The precious words of Divine Reve-

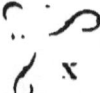

lation were read; fervent prayer was offered; we looked once more on the face of the sleeper, and then turned slowly away, happy in the thought that we were not leaving MARY there; SHE was in heaven.

BARON STOW.

BOSTON, March, 1861.

CONTENTS.

Chapter Fourth.

Chapter Fifth.

Chapter Sixth.

Chapter Seventh.

LITTLE MARY.

Chapter First.

THE CHILDHOOD OF LITTLE MARY — HER SENSE OF SIN —
LETTERS.

THERE is a portrait of little Mary lying
before me as I write, which recalls her
to my memory more vividly than any
other of the keepsakes which her friends
have preserved. It was taken when she
was but five years old, but it represents
her as I shall always remember her; for
she preserved much of that innocence
and artlessness which we love in infants

to the very close of her brief life, and the sun has stamped that look of innocence upon the burnished plate, as if he loved to help us remember it. Could you glance at the picture, you would see a little, chubby girl, with blue eyes and waving brown hair, with dimpled hands clasped carelessly in her lap, seated in an old-fashioned carved chair. You would be delighted at her beauty. Perhaps you would ask, as many have done, " Is it a *real* picture ? was there ever so gentle and lovable a little girl ? " And we might answer, " Yes, the likeness is perfect. Our little Mary was as gentle and lovable as this."

As she grew older she was still beautiful: she manifested the same gentle and loving spirit. I do not think she was a *perfect* child, for I doubt if there are any perfect children. It is Jesus only, you know, who from infancy " increased in wisdom and stature, and in favor with God and man." Mary was often ill, and then she was sometimes irritable and exacting. I am afraid, too, that when she saw her tall, graceful form and her delicate features in the glass, or overheard the foolish praises of strangers, she sometimes felt that she was beautiful. I don't think Jesus of Nazareth ever did that, though I doubt not he was more beautiful than any little boy you have ever seen ; but it is a very common fault in little children now, and most persons would think it quite pardonable. And it is pardonable ; but only God can pardon irritability and pride.

I have told you of these little faults,
because I want to tell the truth, even
about those whom I love very dearly.
Now, I must tell you of Mary's virtues,
that you may learn to love her as I do.
You could not have helped loving her
had you known her, for everybody loved
Mary. She was herself so gentle and
loving, that she won the hearts of all
who knew her. We used to call her
" the light of. the household ; " but even
her dearest friends did not realize how
like a sunbeam she was, till now, when
the clouds have snatched her from their
sight. Yet I can never forget the tenderness and grace with which she used
to cling to her father when he seated
himself, wearied with thought, in his
big arm-chair; nor how truthful and

obedient she was; nor that a single word was enough for her correction when she had done wrong. But Mary seldom did wrong. The prayers which she learned when a baby at her mother's knee she used to repeat every night; and the Sabbath was a holy day to her. Thus she honored God, and perhaps God honored her in helping her to live so gentle and loving a life; for he has said, "Them that honor me I will honor;" and God always keeps his word. I remember now how we used to smile at the childish earnestness which little Mary used sometimes to manifest to be a Christian. Perhaps we did wrong to smile, and she knew better than we did what God wanted of her; indeed, parents often err in thinking that their children are too young to love the blessed Jesus. Mary dreaded death, as most children do, and she wanted Jesus to take that feeling of dread away. I am writing this little book to tell you how Jesus did this for her, and how he will do it for . you, if you really want him to.

Perhaps you think, "I don't want him to, now. I don't think these terribly good children are very happy." But you *will* want him to by and by, and perhaps when you are ready Jesus won't be. You know the Bible says, "Remember now thy Creator in the days of thy youth, while the evil days come not, nor the years draw nigh when thou shalt say, I have no pleasure in them." Besides, good children are the happiest children in the world. Little Mary was always a good child, and she was always merry and joyful, as good folks ought to be. After she had learned to love Jesus, she was the happiest little girl I ever saw, though she was in great pain, and expecting every day to die. She felt that she should be happy forever in heaven, which is far better than all the happiness that earth can give.

Mary was so gentle, and truthful, and good, that I should hardly have felt like telling her that she was a sinner, though I knew that even little children "are by nature children of wrath;" that is, they are sinners, and must be punished for their sins, unless they are pardoned by Jesus. I should hardly have felt like reminding our good little Mary of this, though I knew it to be true, even of her;

but there was no need of my doing this. One Sunday night, — it was March 11, 1860, — Mary's mother called me into her room. The little girl had been ill for many days then, but was better, and we had no idea that she would not soon be well and strong. I found her in tears; and, taking her in my lap, I asked her what ailed her. She told me that she wanted to be a Christian. O! how glad I was to hear her say that, and how bitterly I felt that I had more cause to weep for my sins than she for hers! I pointed her to " the Lamb of God, who taketh away the sins of the world." I told her how able and how willing Jesus was to save her; how he longed to have her become a Christian. At her request, I read and prayed with her; but nothing seemed to give her comfort. Still the tears rolled down her cheeks, and her whole frame trembled, as she exclaimed: "O! it seems as if I was *such* a sinner that God could n't pardon ME!" How it startled me to think that the finger of God was writing such truths as that on the heart of a child who was so good and gentle; but I felt that it was God's work, and I dared only say to her that Jesus could save the vilest sinners: that he died *on purpose* to do this.

After Mary's death, I found a letter from one of her playmates among her papers, which may, perhaps, have been the first thing which made her feel as if she wanted to be a Christian. I want to thank the little girl who wrote it, and I mean to quote a part of her letter, that you may see how faithful a friend little Mary had. " I believe that Eddie C. is to be baptized next Sunday. He is quite young, but it is very pleasant to think of his being a Christian in his youthful days. I trust that he may enjoy many happy years in trying to follow in his Saviour's footsteps; and it has been my prayer, dear Mary, that some time I might see you brought to the Saviour, pleading for your sins that they might be forgiven. Will you not, my dear Mary, pray that your sins may be forgiven, and come to Christ, and *try to live a better life than I do ?*"

On the day after my conversation with Mary, I returned to my studies; but the next day I sent her, at her request, a nice large Bible, with a letter, from which I shall insert a few sentences, because they were as true of any other little boy or girl as they were of little Mary. "I believe, my dear sister, that Jesus loves you, and wants you to give your heart to him. I know that you want to love him, and want to feel that he is *your* Saviour. Why can't you come to Jesus in prayer, and tell him that you want to love him, and mean to, but you don't know how, and want him to help you? Give yourself up to him ; just as the little boy, of whom I was telling you, jumped into his father's arms when his father called him and told him that it was safe to jump, though he could n't see him. But one thing, my dear sister, *Jesus won't help you unless you mean to be his when you are well as well as when you*

are ill ; and you must give yourself up to
him heartily and thoroughly. O, it is
so blessed to feel that the dear Saviour
loves you ! and I want you to feel this."

Mary received another letter soon after
this, which says such precious things
about Jesus, that I want a part of it to
go into my little book, though I know
that many folks think letter-reading dull
business. Here it is: " Yes, the dear
Jesus died for little Mary. In all his
agony and suffering, he thought of that
little girl he was going to save from
death. You can, darling, if you will,
take all the precious promises in the
Bible to yourself. Christ meant them
for *you.* He meant to be *your* Saviour,
your Comforter, *your* Shepherd. He sees
little Mary, a poor, weak little lamb,

that needs the tenderest care, and he wants to take her up and carry her in his own bosom, where she shall be safe from all harm; where the rude winds will not blow upon her, and where she shall gain strength to live in this world; and then, by and by, he will lead her beside the still waters and into green pastures in heaven. Won't Mary let the dear Jesus do all this for her? He is longing now for this dear little girl to let him take her to be his own loved child. She need n't wait a minute. Jesus' arms are open wide to receive his lost darling, though she has often slighted him and grieved him; all that Mary has to do is to throw herself into them. Can't she do this?"

Chapter Second.

HEALTH BUT NOT HOPE — THE YOUNG INQUIRER AND THE
AGED SAINT — A SUMMER AMONG THE MOUNTAINS.

MANY weeks passed after my first interview with little Mary before I had
much more serious conversation with
her. Much of the time I was away
from home, and when I met the little
sufferer I contented myself with drop-
ping now and then a word which should
assure her that I could not be satisfied
till I felt that she was a Christian. I
knew that Mary had better and wiser
counsellors than I. There was one in

particular to whom Mary seemed to
cling with especial tenderness, and who
I was sure would labor and pray without
ceasing to bring this little lamb to the
great Shepherd of Israel. I felt that
Mary's Aunty O'Brien — for so she loved
to call her, though she was no more
Mary's aunt than she is the aunt of
every child who is seeking Jesus — could
do more for the little girl than I. I
loved to know that little Mary, whenever
she was able to go out for a drive, would
send her carriage for her good aunty;
and O, it was a precious sight to see
the pale and anxious face of the little
girl nestling down among the furs beside
her old and gentle and heavenly-minded
friend, and think that they were talking
of the blessed Jesus. I knew they were

talking of Jesus, because Aunty O'Brien talks so sweetly and so winningly of Jesus to every one whom she meets; because she had often talked to me about Jesus, and led me, I hope, to love him and try to serve him. I saw that little Mary had not lost her interest in such conversation as this. I felt that the blessed Spirit was still striving to win her to Christ, and I could not help feeling that she *would be* a Christian.

All this time Mary was slowly getting better. The frosts of winter were gone; the fields were fresh and green, the birds sang sweetly in the maples under Mary's window, and all nature seemed to be praising the good God who has made this beautiful world for man to live in. As the warm days of summer drew near, the roses bloomed on Mary's cheeks brighter than ever, and we hoped she was past all danger. Still, we knew she was delicate and frail, and her father made his plans to shut up his house in the hot and dusty city, and have his family spend the whole summer among the mountains of Mary's native state. We were all of us glad to go, for we loved the mountains, and you would love them too, if you knew them well. Just think of living all summer in a little green valley, not more than an eighth of a mile wide, hemmed in on every side by lofty mountains covered to the very top with waving trees, — as if Boston Common were surrounded by hills ten times as high as the steeple of Park-street Church, and you were to have your home on the little knoll by the Frog Pond! And think of the beautiful lakes and laughing waterfalls; the grand Old Man of the Mountain, which God carved out of the solid rock, thousands of feet up on the mountain side, so that it looks just like a man's face! Think of the rattling stage-coaches, filled with happy travellers; the Indian encampments, the pleasant walks, and drives, and sails, and you will not wonder that we were glad to go to our mountain home.

But there were two things for which I most wanted to go to the mountains. I hoped that the fine, clear, bracing air would restore little Mary to perfect health; and I remembered that God had said, "The mountains shall bring peace to the people," and I longed to have them bring peace to Mary's troubled heart. In both my wishes I was disappointed. At first the change of air and scene seemed to give her new life, and little Mary never looked so beautiful as in that last summer among " the Crystal Hills." But we soon learned that the glow which suffused her cheeks was not the bloom of health. The bustle and tumult of a crowded hotel seemed to weary her, and she gradually lost the little strength which she had gained. We were more anxious than ever for our darling. And I was more anxious about her immortal soul than her frail body, dearly as I loved her, and eagerly as I prayed that she might be " the light of our home " for many years. Little

Mary had never felt that she was a
Christian, and it seemed to me that she
was not reading her Bible so regularly,
or praying so often, or seeking Christ so
earnestly, as in the weeks that were past.
Perhaps she was discouraged by not finding Jesus when she first set out to seek
him, and did not know that the blessed
Saviour sometimes lets folks search for
him a great while, so as to make sure
that they *really* want to find him, and
that they will not grow weary of serving
him when they have found him. Perhaps the gayety and bustle of the hotel
distracted her childish thoughts. Perhaps she could not quite make up her
mind to give up everything for Jesus; for
he wants his followers to give up many
things which look very bright and pleas-

ant to a little girl like Mary, though he
gives them many more and better gifts
in exchange. I think this last was the
reason why little Mary did not find Jesus
sooner. God was all this time calling
her to himself. She heard his voice ;
but many weeks of pain and anguish
must pass before Mary could give up all
to Christ, and say, like little Samuel,
" Speak, Lord, for thy servant heareth."

As the summer passed away, little
Mary grew more and more feeble. Her
voice was heard no more upon the piazza
and along the halls. Her sweet smile
no longer won the hearts of strangers in
the crowded parlor. I read in a paper
published in a distant city these kind
and loving words, and wept when I
thought that the true-hearted pastor who

wrote them was speaking of little Mary, and despairing of her life :

" In the house of mirth and gladness there is a chamber of sickness. Opposite the room in which we write is one, well known to many of your readers, a frail flower, lovely to her friends. Around her suffering couch hangs a watchful, sympathizing mother, and friendly hands are extended to minister to her relief. Patiently she bears what God has laid upon her, hoping that, in his kindness, he will bring back the bloom to her faded cheek, and health to her wasted form. Beautiful lesson taught us, who are so happy and joyous, that we are to have all our earthly joys chastened by the thought that this is not our final and perfect rest. Beyond and above the everlasting hills there is a Paradise, into which no pain enters, and upon the fair flowers of which no blight ever falls."

Still the little sufferer failed, and at last it was decided that the only hope of her recovery lay in her removal to the quiet of her distant home, though many feared that the little heart which thumped so wildly would cease its beating altogether before her journey's end. Strong arms and tender hearts bore the wasted form of little Mary from her bedside to the carriage which waited to convey her to the railroad, twelve miles away, and laid her gently upon the rude couch which was prepared for her. O! it was a touching sight to see her borne away, — so frail, so feeble; and eyes unused to weep shed genuine tears as the carriage drove from the door with its precious freight.

Little Mary reached the cars in safety, and was soon whirled along, down peaceful valleys, beneath the shadow of overhanging mountains, along the margin of placid lakes, to her far-off home. O, what a contrast there was between the quiet loveliness of the untroubled landscape, glowing beneath the fierce rays of the August sun, and the gloom and anxiety which reigned within that silent car! But loving and skilful friends were watching over little Mary, and the great and tender God watched over her and stayed her up. He soothed her pain, and helped her to endure fatigue, for he meant to spare our darling till he had done great things for her and for us.

Towards nightfall the cars shot across the clear blue waters of the Merrimac, and wound swiftly though the elm-shaded intervales which encircle our beautiful city, and Mary was home again. Her heart beat with a thrill of joy as she was borne to the quiet chamber where she was to suffer and to enjoy so much; for she felt that she was coming home to die, and she could not bear to die among strangers.

Chapter Third.

HOPES AND FEARS—SONGS IN THE NIGHT—THE BRUISED REED AND THE SMOKING FLAX.

WE had hoped that little Mary's removal to her quiet home might be the means of her recovery; but the change did not seem to do her much good. She was certainly happier, and more comfortable in her own dear home than she could be anywhere else. Sometimes she would seem to be really better for a few days, and as she sat propped up in. her easy-chair, with a basket of golden fruit by her side, and a book in her

hand, as the old sweet smile came back
to her worn face, we felt quite hopeful. Then her disease would assume
a new form, and she would seem so
much worse that we would give up all
thoughts of her recovery. But still the
doctors told us that Mary might be well
again, and we clung to their words of
encouragement long after our own hearts
told us that she must die.

All this while little Mary was suffering
the severest pain. Perhaps you have not
suffered so much in all your life put
together as she suffered every day for
months. Yet she was very gentle and
patient. I have told you before that she
used sometimes to be peevish and exacting when she was sick. She seemed so
different now, that I could n't help

thinking, sometimes, that God might already have given her a new heart. But I never said so to her, for I could not be sure of this; and I felt that it would do her more harm to think that she was a Christian when she was not, than to be a Christian for a little while without knowing it. By and by I had no occasion to tell her that I hoped she was a Christian, and every one who saw her patience and gentleness under much severer pain felt that she was wonderfully and beautifully changed. When folks are really Christians, they will soon find it out, and others will find it out too, without any one to tell them.

There was one thing which helped little Mary very much to bear her pain

during all her illness. She was very
fond of music; and sometimes, when she
was suffering a great deal, she would
want her kind aunts, who took care of
her, to sing to her all night long.
" Sing! sing! " she would exclaim, when
a sudden pang shot through her heart;
and as they bent over her, and asked her
what they should sing, she would often
answer:

> " O, sing to me of heaven,
>   When I 'm about to die ! "

She loved best to have *hymns* sung by
her bedside, and would herself pick out
such hymns as were not only set to the
sweetest melody, but full of the deepest
and tenderest thoughts about Jesus.
One night, when Mary's mother, over-

come by fatigue, had fallen asleep by her
side, she asked a kind Christian woman
who was watching with her to sing her
some hymns. The good woman tried to
sing, but Mary's sensitive ear was not
satisfied. "I'll wind up the music-box,"
said Mrs. L., — for Mary had a fine large
music-box, which she loved to hear, and
which was often playing when her watchers were tired of singing. "Why, no!"
replied Mary, with surprise, "it's Sunday!" Dearly as she loved the gentle
melody of her music-box, she would not
hear it even for a moment on the Sabbath, and she did not think, as many
little girls do, that Sunday was over
when folks get home from meeting in
the afternoon. So she tried to sing
herself. At first her voice was weak

and broken, but she gathered strength as she reached the verse:

"I would not live alway; no — welcome the tomb:
Since Jesus hath lain there, I dread not its gloom;
There sweet be my rest till he bid me arise
To hail him in triumph descending the skies."

And it seemed as if heavenly voices blended with hers in divinest harmony. She sung the whole hymn through, and then turned to Mrs. L. and said: " O, it must be sweet to be a Christian! " " It is sweet, darling," replied her faithful watcher. " O, how I wish I was one! " answered little Mary. Then she talked with Mrs. L. about her own unconverted children, and urged her to pray more that her boys might be brought to Christ.

Perhaps you think that little Mary must have been a Christian even now. Sometimes I thought so, but I was not quite satisfied. I wanted *her* to feel that she was a Christian. I used often to read the Bible to her, and pray with her, and so did her kind pastor. She would very frequently ask us to mark a passage which pleased her, so that she could find it herself. She always listened with respectful attention when prayer was offered, or anything said to her; but she herself said but little; and we could not talk with her quite as we wished, for it was feared that if she was excited at all, her recovery might be hindered. Besides, some of her friends seemed to think that little Mary had always been so good and gentle that it

would be well with her if she were
taken away, whether she was a Christian or not. I loved to think of her
gentle and guileless childhood as much
as any one, and I knew that God was
very merciful to little children; but I
felt that the only way to heaven was
through the blood of Jesus. I remembered how bitterly little Mary had felt
that she needed a Saviour, and I could
not help thinking that if she was old
enough to feel her need of him, she
was old enough to believe in him, and
love him. Sometimes I was afraid that
because she did not give her heart right
to God when he seemed to want it so
much, he was n't going to take it at
all. I felt very sad and very anxious.
I did n't expect great things from a

little child like Mary; but I wanted to
see her clinging to the blessed Saviour
with the same childish confidence and
love which she felt towards her dear
father. Then I should know that she
was ready to die, because she was fit to
live.

On Sunday, September 30, I spent an
hour in Mary's room, reading and praying, and talking with her. I told her
how ready the dear Saviour was, when
he was on earth, to heal all those whom
he met. I read to her the account of
that beautiful scene where they brought
unto Jesus, as the sun was setting, all
that were diseased, and the *whole city*
was gathered together at the door, and
he healed many. I told her that he was
just as near, just as strong, and just as

willing to save, *now*, as when he was on earth. I told her how gentle and loving he is, and then said: " Dear Mary, can't you love and trust such a Saviour as this?" She looked steadily in my face for a moment, while two tears stole down her cheeks, — the only tears which I saw her shed during her long illness, — and answered, " Why, I do *love* him, now." I felt, from the emphasis which the little girl laid on the word *love*, that she had an idea that *trusting* in Jesus was a very difficult and complicated matter. So I tried to make her feel how simple a thing it is to trust in Jesus ; that we have only to feel that he is able and willing to save us, and so give ourselves up to him, and let him do just what he pleases with us ; that we must trust in the blessed Jesus, just as we trust in our kind and loving parents, feeling that they know what is best for us, and will do what is best, whether we understand it all or not.

I was a good deal encouraged by my talk with Mary. It seemed to me that she did *love* Jesus. I remembered the words of the prophet: "A bruised reed shall he not break, and smoking flax shall he not quench;" that is, Jesus will accept the service even of the weakest and humblest if they really try to serve him. I thought, surely God will accept even thus much of faith and love from a little child, so weak and sick, too. But I did not remember *all* of God's glorious promise. It is: "A bruised reed shall he not break, and smoking flax shall he not quench, *till he bring forth judgment unto* VICTORY." But God remembered it all. He had indeed accepted little Mary, but he was preparing a VICTORY for her such as I never had dreamed of, and would never have dared to ask. I never knew what VICTORY meant till I had seen little Mary die; and then, O, how grateful I was that God had taught me this lesson over the death-bed of my own sister!

The next day I returned to my studies, but not till little Mary had charged me to pray for her while I was gone, and bade me summon her Aunty O'Brien to take my place by her bedside. Mary had many loving friends, who were always ready to talk with her about Jesus, and she loved dearly to

have them all with her; but there were
two or three whom she seemed especially to want, now that she was seeking
Christ.

Chapter Fourth.

VICTORY — A HAPPY SABBATH — WATCHING FOR SOULS.

DURING the early part of October there seemed to be no marked change in Mary's condition. She was gradually failing, and I think she felt this as keenly as her friends, though she did not speak of it. She still seemed to delight in the singing of her favorite hymns, and often asked to have the Bible read and prayer offered by her bedside. If we asked what we should pray for, her answer almost always was, " That I may be patient." Poor child ! she seemed to

dread more than anything else that her
intense pain would betray her into impa-
tience or fretfulness; but the prayers for
patience were wonderfully answered, and
never did I see a sweeter or more gentle
sufferer. But, O! I longed to hear her
talk more of the Lord Jesus, so that I
might know how he seemed to her in
this trying hour. And God meant to
satisfy my longings to the full.

On Saturday morning, October 20, she
asked her Aunt Maria if she thought she
would ever get well. She replied, "I
don't know, Mary; you are very sick."
She then said, "Tell mother, if I don't
get well, to give Johnnie my Bible, and
have some one write in it that hymn,

'See Israel's gentle Shepherd stand,
    With all-engaging charms.'

Some days after she repeated this request, adding, " I promised Aunty O'Brien once that I would learn that hymn ; but I never did it, and I am heartily ashamed of myself." Later in the day, she said to her mother: " O dear ! I am afraid I shall never be well again. Do you think I shall, mother ? " Her mother told her that we hoped so, but that it was very doubtful. She then asked to see her dear pastor, and he was summoned to her side. I will let him describe the scene which followed, in his own words : " Leaning over her, I said, ' My dear child, what would you have me do ? Raising herself, in her weakness, from her sick-bed, she threw her arm around my neck, and, in the most tender and earnest tones, said, ' O, I want to be good!' I tried to meet that desire, so touchingly expressed, by telling her of the nature and mission of Jesus. As I ceased speaking, she said, 'I *will* trust in Jesus!' and she did, and found him precious to her soul."

That earnest decision was the turning-point with little Mary. She had long felt that she loved Jesus, but the world seemed bright and joyous to a little girl like her, and she had not been quite willing to give up everything for him, and let him do with her just what he pleased. Now she gave up all to Christ, and he gave her in exchange "the peace of God which passeth all understanding." Is it not a good exchange for a little girl to make? From this time her perfect resignation and trust were apparent to all. She said to her mother, "You will soon learn not to miss me, mother." Her mother's answer was, "No, Mary, this can never seem like home without you." — "Well, mother," she replied, "I mean, if it is God's will, you are willing that I should go, ain't you?" It was hard to say yes; but long before she died we had learned to pray that she might soon find rest from her sufferings in the bosom of that Saviour whom she so much loved.

This Saturday was a day of intense agony for little Mary, but it was a day of constant prayer. She asked every one who entered her sick-room to pray with her; and lips unused to prayer caught the inspiration of the little sufferer, and poured out their full hearts in fervent petitions unto God. To borrow the words of her kind pastor: "She might be said to live in an atmosphere of prayer. It seemed ever to soothe her pain, and to yield happiness to her spirit. Such delight in oft-repeated prayer, and so firm a reliance on its efficacy, I have rarely seen, even in the most mature Christian. Hers was indeed a child-like trust. She seemed to take the Saviour at his word, and make him her 'all and in all.' As her outer life waned, her spiritual life grew stronger and stronger, and prayer was the medium by which that spiritual life was communicated to the soul."

During this day she often asked her father, whom perhaps she loved best of all her friends, to pray with her. He

would kneel by her side and try to pray;
but, overcome by his emotions, his voice
choked, and he could not utter a word.
Once, when he rose hastily from his
knees and left the room, she said, " Tell
father not to feel so badly; tell him I
am willing to go." That was indeed a
comfort; but it is hard to soothe the sor-
rows of a father's heart as he bends over
the death-bed of his moaning child, even
by such blessed assurance as this.

The next day was the Sabbath, a day
of the severest pain, but, as Mary told
one of her kind watchers at its close, the
happiest day of her life. It was a happy
day for little Mary, because Jesus was
very near her, and every little girl is
happy who has Jesus for her friend.
Towards nightfall, as she sat upon the

side of her bed, with her pale face leaning upon her father's shoulder, and his
strong arms round her, she exclaimed
to her sister: "We're *so* happy! ain't we,
Kate?" Then, looking up in her father's
face, and seeing that he was in tears, she
added: "We are *all* happy, ain't we,
father? Ain't you *happy*, father? You
must be happy." The little girl had
caught the spirit of those beautiful
words,

> "Since He is mine, and I am His,
> What *can* I want besides?"

She felt that every one who loved Jesus,
and whom Jesus loved, *must* be happy.

And there was one other thing which
made this a happy Sabbath for Mary.
She had been working for Jesus. What!

you say, a little girl so weak and sick
working for Jesus? Yes. Every one
who really loves him will work for Jesus.
They can't help it. They will find a
chance somehow. You remember how,
when Jesus was on earth, and Andrew
had seen him, he ran at once and found
his own brother Peter, and told him that
he had found Christ; and Peter soon
found him too. Andrew never did very
much for Jesus, but Peter, you know,
did a great deal; and, perhaps, if it had
not been for Andrew, Peter would never
have found the Lord. So little Mary,
weak and sick as she was, and so soon
to die, could not do much work for
Jesus herself, but perhaps she could
call some one to his service who might
work long and hard for the blessed Mas-

ter. At any rate, she called her own
brother Johnnie to her on this bright
Sunday morning, just as Andrew called
Peter, and told him that she had found
Christ. She loved Johnnie very much,
and played with him a great deal when
she was well; and now she wanted him
to love Jesus. She told him that he
must be a good boy, and not wait till he
was sick before he loved the Saviour, as
she had done. She reminded him that
he was to have her Bible after she was
gone, and said: "I don't give you my
Bible to lay up, Johnnie; I give it to you
to read."

Mary spoke of her brother Frank,
too, who was away at school, saying:
"I should think that Frank was old
enough"— Here she stopped, either

because she was in so much pain, or
because she didn't quite know how to
finish the sentence. Her mother asked,
" Should you think Frank was old
enough to love the Saviour ? " — " Yes,"
replied Mary, " and he don't know how
pleasant it is." She longed to have her
whole family meet her in heaven, and
seemed to be willing even to die that she
might lead them to Christ. Often she
urged them to live near to Jesus ; and
one day, when her mother said to her,
" Mary, I don't know what your father
will do without you ; he has always
idolized you," she answered, " I know
it, mother ; perhaps that is why I am
taken."

Little Mary was not satisfied with
working for Christ only a single day.

From this time till the close of her life she "watched for souls as one that must give account." Her last message to the children of the Sabbath school was, "Tell them to love Jesus, and meet me in heaven;" and many of them wept over her message after their little sister, "so mild and lovely," was laid in the silent grave. Towards one of her little playmates she was especially faithful. We have a little girl in Concord whom we call "our little missionary girl," because her father and mother are far away over the deep blue sea, trying to teach the little heathen children about Jesus. Mary loved this little girl very much, and one day she sent for her to come and see her. After she had gone home, Mary seemed very sad, and said to her mother, "I wanted to see Mary S. alone." So the next day the little missionary girl was summoned to her bedside again, and Mary had a long talk with her. I do not know what she said, but I know that Mary S. went home sobbing as if her heart would break, and saying, "I have promised little Mary G. to meet her in heaven."

This happy Sabbath of which I have been telling you was begun and ended with prayer. When Mary's watchers entered the room at night, she said, "O, Mrs. D., will you pray with me?"—"I will try to, Mary," she replied; "what shall I pray for?" Mary's answer was, "That I may be a good girl, and love the Saviour." May that be the prayer of every child who reads this little book.

"Let me love thee more and more,
If I love at all, I pray :
If I never loved before,
Help me to begin to-day."

Chapter Fifth.

WAITING FOR DELIVERANCE.

On the following Monday we told
Mary that we had sent for Dr. Bowditch,
of Boston, to come up and see her.
Her first thought was, "Is he a Christian?" She seemed throughout her illness to be very grateful to her physicians
for their tenderness and care; but we
could see that she would have been happier if she could have been in charge of
one who might at the same time have
ministered to the body and the soul.
On the arrival of Dr. B. he gave us

some encouragement to hope for Mary's recovery, and we told her of this, but it seemed to awaken very little hope in her own breast. During all this week she suffered much, yet seemed to be clinging to Jesus, and confident that " the great Physician " could do much more for her than any human helper.

On Wednesday her brother was at home, and read and prayed with her. She was very weak, and he feared that the service would weary her; but she said, " No, I love to hear you. I am too tired to talk, but I want you to sit by my side and talk to me." He remained by her bedside, rubbing her swollen limbs, and repeating a few verses from the Bible. or from her favorite hymns, and now and then uttering a few words

of prayer. She seemed to delight in
listening, and once, as he was speaking
of the attractions of heaven, and said,
" Sometimes heaven seems so glorious,
and Jesus so precious, that I feel as if
we could n't go to him too soon," she
interrupted him with the words, " That
is the way it seems to me." Later in
the day, our former pastor, Dr. Stow,
visited the little sufferer, and read and
prayed with her. As he rose from his
knees, he asked her if she did not want
to get well. She looked him calmly
in the face, and answered, " If it is the
will of the Lord Jesus, I *should* like to
get well ; but I am not afraid to die. I
think I should go to be with Jesus."

Dr. S. saw her but for a few moments,
at a time when she was so much under

the influence of powerful medicines that
she did not seem to us like herself; but
he was deeply impressed with the loveliness of her Christian character. After
little Mary's body was laid in the grave,
he wrote to her father: "The maid is
not dead, but sleepeth. She sleeps in
Jesus. Her spirit, released from a body
of pain and protracted agony, rests in
the bosom of her Saviour. You have
joy in the departure of your Mary, the
sweetest solace you could have in any
case. She was the best prepared of any
of you for an exchange of worlds.
Jesus wanted just that flower from your
garden to deck the paradise on high.
There she blooms in imperishable beauty
and fragrance. No autumnal frosts can
reach her there. Safe home! May you

all so live that you may as safely finish
your appointed course, and be forever
with her in the better land."

On Sunday evening Mary seemed to
revive a little, and sent for her pastor,
who came and talked with her about
heaven, a theme which never failed to
interest her. As he told her that there
would be no pain there, and expressed
the hope that soon they might both join
the angels in singing the praises of God,
she exclaimed, with childish earnestness,
"O, won't that be *nice!*" The next
day Dr. Bowditch visited Mary again,
and found her failing fast. After he
was gone, she said to her aunt, "I guess
Dr. Bowditch didn't give you much
encouragement this time?" On being
frankly told that he did not, she added,

" Aunt Nancy, I *am* a little bit afraid to
die, — *only just a little bit.*" But the
next day even that little cloud which
obscured the sunshine of her faith was
gone. Her grandmother came to bid
her a last good-by, and said, " Mary, I
hope I shall meet you in heaven."
— " You must *be sure and come there,*
grandmother, and tell grandfather to
come too." — " Mary is not afraid to
die?" said her mother. " No!" exclaimed
the little girl, with wonderful earnestness, " not a *speck* afraid." Then, after
her mother had left the room, she turned
to Mrs. P., and said, " Sometimes it
seems as if I could n't wait." It was
very touching, during this last interview
between the aged grandmother and her
dying namesake, to hear the little girl

say, "Grandmother, if there are any of my things which you want after I am gone, you shall have them." Now, as ever, she was more thoughtful of others than herself.

All hope of Mary's recovery was now abandoned, and her mother said to her, "Darling, if you must go, I should love to go with you." — "O, no!" she exclaimed, as if horror-stricken at the thought, "you must stay and comfort father." It was touching to see how tenderly she clung to him to the very end of life. She seemed to have something which she wanted very much to say to him; but whenever she tried to speak, his tears and sobs interrupted her. At last her mother said to her, "If you have anything which you would like your father to do, tell me what it is, and it shall be done." — "TELL HIM TO LIVE NEAR THE SAVIOUR," was her answer. It was a simple message, but it was enough. The faithful and loving wife had pledged her husband to their dying child "to live near the Saviour," and Mary could die happy.

But Mary not only thought of her father; she thought of all her friends, and tried even in little things to make them happy. "Mother," she said, "I should like to have Kate and William and the baby come over and spend the day, *if it would not be too much trouble for you.*" I am afraid that many little girls who are strong and well are not so thoughtful of their mother's comfort. And why do you think she wanted these friends to visit her? She wanted William and Kate to pray with her. A week before she had said to her mother, " Do you think William *would* pray with me if I asked him?" She seemed to retain her delight in prayer and song to the very last. Indeed, this was never more touchingly shown than on the last Wednesday she spent on earth.

On the morning of that day her pastor came in, and sat by her bedside for a long time, but, as Mary seemed to be in great distress, did not offer to pray with her. At last she turned to him and said, " Why don't you pray, Mr. Flanders?" He replied, " I have been praying all this time, Mary." — " Why don't you pray aloud?" — " Because I was afraid it would tire you." — " O no," she replied, " I would like a short prayer, but you must not mind if I get to sleep." He knelt down and offered a brief petition. As he rose, she exclaimed, " I want more ! " — " More what ? " said her mother. " More prayer." O that older Christians had such a longing for the throne of grace as little Mary had! She did indeed want " more prayer." Her brother Eddie, her mother, her aunts, her sisters, — all who came in, — were permitted to share in the precious privilege of praying by her bedside. When Mrs. L. came to watch with her, Mary at once said, " Pray ; " and the good woman *did* pray, as if the gates of heaven were open before her, and the dear Saviour stood ready to snatch each sentence, as it fell from her lips, and present it as sweet incense unto God. When she was done, Mary said, "Take the chair at which Mrs. L. knelt and place it beside the bed, with a pillow on it, so that I can lean against it." It was done, and she sat upon the bedside for some minutes, leaning against the chair in an attitude of devotion, and saying, "Now I can pray myself." The exertion wearied her, and she was soon obliged to lie down again. After she was settled in bed, she said to her mother, "Mother, I could n't collect my thoughts." — "You need not collect them, darling; a single thought is enough," was her mother's reply. And it was a beautiful and true reply. No little child must think, because she cannot offer such prayers as her father or her pastor do, that God will not hear and answer. He loves the prayers of little children.

During the same day she asked her sister Bidie to give her the book which Mrs. Flanders had sent her, and insisted on finding for herself a hymn which had been marked, though the effort evidently wearied her very much. The book was "Songs in the Night," and the hymn is called, "Go and tell Jesus." When Mary had found it, she asked her sister to read it to her. Then she wished her to read another hymn, and Bidie selected

"When languor and disease invade
This trembling house of clay,"

and read it through. You may read it for yourself, and see how full of precious thoughts it is for a little girl who feels that she is soon to die. Mary then wanted her sister to go down in the parlor and play on the piano. She played "Evan;" and, as the melody floated sweetly upward to the sick-room, Mary herself began to sing,

"O for a closer walk with God!
  A calm and heavenly frame!
A light to shine upon the road
  Which leads me to the Lamb!"

The melody then changed to the "Shining Shore," and as the little sufferer recognized the tune, she exclaimed, "I can see it! I can see it!" Perhaps she could, for she was certainly very near to heaven.

Little Mary not only delighted in

prayer and praise, but she longed for the house of God. On this last Wednesday, when so many little girls were playing with their dolls, or rolling their hoops in the bright sunshine, our happy little Mary lay, in her darkened room, on a bed of pain. Don't you think she longed to be out in the clear, cool air? O, yes! and I will tell you why. "Mother," she said, "I should like to go to church once more. When Harry comes home, can't we have him preach a sermon in this room? It would be so pleasant to have a meeting here." And then she added, "Mother, I wish you would have Frank and Johnnie go to meeting all day. I don't love to have them go only half a day." It would have been a precious privilege to me to

have preached from the words, "O
Death, where is thy sting? O Grave,
where is thy victory?" within that quiet
room; and her mother promised little
Mary that I should, if she were well
enough to hear me. But before I stood
by my darling's side she had grown so
weak and faint that I could only talk to
her in broken sentences of Jesus' love.

Chapter Sixth.

ALMOST HOME — ASLEEP IN JESUS — MOUNT AUBURN.

ON the next morning after this happy Wednesday, we gathered in Mary's room to see her die. She seemed to be suffering more than ever before, and no one thought that her feeble frame could long endure such agony. As her weeping friends bent over her, eager to catch the last words which fell from their darling's lips, she opened her full, bright eyes, turned languidly towards her mother, and motioned for water. A glass was filled and offered, but she turned away.

Summoning her strength, as for a last effort, she exclaimed, "Let *father* give it to me." Like the blessed Saviour, she loved her own unto the end. As the strong man bent in speechless anguish over his darling child, and pressed the tumbler to her pallid lips, more than one of us recalled the promise, " Whosoever shall give to one of these little ones a cup of cold water only, shall in no wise lose his reward." We prayed that the loving father might be rewarded manifold for his tender care of the dying child.

God's time for the deliverance of little Mary had not yet come. Powerful remedies relieved her pain, and seemed to give her a new hold on life ; but it was not the life in which we had so delighted. Her mind was clouded, and seemed sometimes to wander. Still she knew and loved us all; and, best of all, she knew and loved her Saviour. It wearied her to talk; but she loved to listen to those who spoke of the Lamb of God; and it was evident, from her answers to their inquiries, that *Jesus* was still precious to her, and heaven a near and pleasant reality. I do not think there was a single day in which she did not ask for prayer, and prayer was freely and fervently offered by her side. Such prayers I had never heard as those which went up to heaven from that chamber of suffering. On Friday her mother asked her if she would like her brother to come in and pray with her. She looked up almost reproachfully, and answered : " Have I not told you many times ? " MORE PRAYER was still her watchword. Once or twice on the following day she asked for singing ; but she was so weak that even her favorite hymns wearied her, and she soon hushed the loving voices which sung of Jesus.

The last Sabbath which little Mary spent on earth was the last day on which all her loved ones were gathered around her bed. We had been in the habit of having family worship, on Sabbath mornings, in Mary's room, since she had been so ill. I do not know whether she realized that it was God's holy day, for she had so fully caught the spirit of heaven, that, as she herself said, " every day seemed like Sunday now." But I think she remembered the day ; for when her mother came into the room, after breakfast, she said : "Turn me over, quick!" and when it was done, added, "Now I suppose we will have prayers." Her mother replied, "Well, I will call Henry, and no one else shall come." — "Why not more?" said Mary. "Because I thought it would weary you," answered her mother. "Do you want them all?" She said, "Yes," and the whole family were summoned to her bedside — oppressed by the thought that never again would they *all* unite on earth in the worship of God. I think it was then that I read Luke's touching narrative of that Jewish ruler who had "one only daughter, *about twelve years of age, and she lay a-dying,*" and, like Jairus of old, "fell down at Jesus' feet and be-

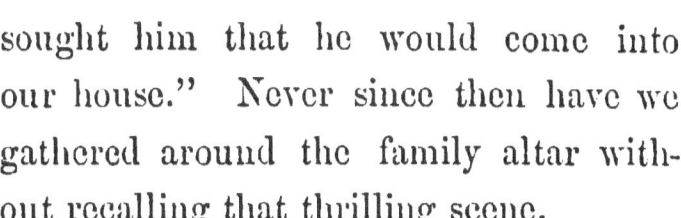

sought him that he would come into
our house." Never since then have we
gathered around the family altar without recalling that thrilling scene.

On Tuesday, November 6, the death
angel was indeed hovering over Mary's
couch, but he came in no gloomy form.
Little Mary had suffered so much during
her illness that we dreaded to think what
the last struggle might be. As she lin-
gered along from day to day, our oft-
repeated question was, "Will the end
be peaceful and quiet?" God was better than our fears. During the morning
of this day Mary lay in a sort of doze.
Once or twice she asked, by signs or
broken words, for "more prayer," and
her pastor and brother led her to the
throne of grace. While the family were

at dinner, her mother remained by Mary's side, and, as she seemed quiet and wakeful, said, " Little Mary is going to heaven. We are the ones to be pitied, darling. You will soon be happy." " Yes," she replied, " it seems as if I could n't wait so long." Then, after a short pause, she looked up earnestly in her mother's face, and added, " O, mother! when? how long?" — " I don't know, darling; soon, I hope," was the reply.

After dinner she seemed to be gradually failing, and in much distress. She talked a great deal, but so indistinctly that we could catch only a word now and then. At last she said, very distinctly, " Why don't somebody talk?" Her mother replied, " We feel so sad, darling, to see you suffer, that we can't talk." Her brother, who was already in the room, now approached the bed, and, laying his hand upon the head of the dying saint, began to repeat brief passages of Scripture, and utter short sentences of prayer or words of comfort and hope. This service continued for perhaps half an hour, and during the whole time not a word or a groan escaped the little sufferer. Her aspect was perfectly tranquil, and the impression left upon her weeping friends was that of peace and joy in the presence of Jesus and the near approach of heaven. Fearing that she might be fatigued, her brother left her side, and her pillows were adjusted so as to render her position more comfortable. When this had been done, she seemed as if something was still wanting to her comfort, and her mother asked, "Do you want Harry to tell you some more about Jesus?" She replied, "*Of course I do;*" and he was recalled to her side. As he entered the room, she said, "Tell me quick, or it will be too late!"—"Dear child," he replied, "you will soon know more about Jesus than we can tell you. You will see Jesus. He will take you in his arms and carry you in his bosom; he will lead you into green pastures and beside still waters; he will bring you to those dear brothers and sisters who have gone before you to heaven, and soon, very soon, some of us will meet you there." Then, throwing his thoughts into the form of prayer, he continued: "Dear

Jesus, we thank thee that when thou
wast on earth thou didst say, 'Suffer
little children to come unto me, and forbid them not.' Here is a little child
who means to take thee at thy word, who
wants to come to thee and say, Blessed
Saviour, here I am"— No one who wit-
nessed the scene can ever forget the earnestness and emphasis with which she
interrupted him at this point, saying,
"*Yes, yes,* that's it!" Again, as he continued in prayer, and was pleading the
precious promise, "When thou passest
through the waters I will be with thee,
and through the rivers they shall not
overflow thee," she tried to speak, ap-
parently desirous to bear witness to the
truth, but her voice failed her. Her
brother leaned over her, and said, "It's

true, is n't it, darling?"—"O, yes," she replied, "but I'm too tired to hear more now."

A few minutes later she called for her brother Johnnie, and he, with Addie, the youngest of the flock, was led to her bedside. "Bring him where I can see him," she said; and the two boys were placed where her eyes fell full upon them. "Now bring them some little chairs — or any chairs." Her request was complied with; and the two boys, seated side by side, with streaming eyes, while their dying sister gazed wistfully and intently at them, and weeping friends thronged the room, presented a scene over which the angels of heaven must have bent with tearful interest. Fearing that she would be unable to

address them herself, so rapidly did she
fail, I passed again to her side, and
placing my hand on her brow, where
the death-sweat was already gathering,
said: "You want them to be good boys,
darling, and love the blessed Saviour?"
— "O, yes!" she said. "And then," I
added, "when they come to die, Jesus
will be near them, to support and comfort them, as he does little Mary."
Again she said, "O, yes!" and, in reply
to further words of consolation, expressed
her consciousness of the presence and
preciousness of the Saviour.

During this last scene her pastor had
entered the room, and I said to him,
"If you would offer a short prayer, I
know it would be acceptable to Mary."
He kneeled by her bedside and uttered

a few words, but she interrupted him, saying, "Not just now; wait a minute; I'm too tired." The time for finishing his prayer never came. From this moment she gradually and gently failed, until, at half-past three, she fell asleep in Jesus,—so peacefully, that for several minutes we could hardly tell whether she was on earth or in heaven. "For so He giveth his beloved sleep." May God grant that little Johnnie and Addie, and many more little children, may be won by her happy life and peaceful death to Jesus' arms.

Three days after our little Mary had fallen asleep in Jesus a sad procession

wound its way through the avenues of
Mount Auburn to lay her body in the
quiet grave. It was a lovely day, and
lovely was the tall, lithe form which lay
in her wreathed casket amid the rustling
leaves. The joyous look of childhood
had chased the traces of pain and sor-
row from her worn features, and strangers even drew near and wept over the
grave of the lovely sleeper. It was a sad
and yet a joyous sight; for we could say,
with no doubtful and faltering accents,
"It is well with the child." Many a
heart murmured Amen as one who
knew little Mary well repeated the
words with which old John Bunyan
introduces the dying Christian to his
heavenly home. "Now, just as the gates
were opened to let in the men, I looked

in after them, and behold, the city shone like the sun; the streets also were paved with gold; and in them walked many men with crowns on their heads, palms in their hands, and golden harps to sing praises withal. There were also some of them that had wings, and they answered one another without intermission, saying, 'Holy, holy, holy is the Lord!' And after that they shut up the gates; which when I had seen, I *wished myself among them.*"

Is this wish yours, dear reader? Let your life and death be that of LITTLE MARY.

"Another hand is beckoning us,
    Another call is given;
And glows once more with angel-steps
    The path which reaches heaven.

"Our young and gentle friend, whose smile
  Made brighter summer hours,
Amid the frost of autumn time
  Has left us with the flowers.

  * * * * *

"Fold her, O Father, in thine arms,
  And let her henceforth be
A messenger of love between .
  Our human hearts and thee.

"Still let her mild rebuking stand
  Between us and the wrong;
And her dear memory serve to make
  Our faith in goodness strong.

"And grant that she who, trembling here,
  Distrusted all her powers,
May welcome to her holier home
  The well-beloved of ours."

Chapter Seventh.

JESUS THE LITTLE CHILDREN'S SAVIOUR.

You have heard a great deal, dear children, about the blessed Saviour whom little Mary loved, who left his home in heaven and became a little child on earth, and then, when he had grown to be a man, did many wonderful works, uttered many precious words, and at last died on Calvary. I hope you are not tired of hearing about him, for I want to tell you that he died for you, and help you, if I can, to love him and serve him. Some folks seem to think

that little children have no need of the
Saviour, and cannot love him if they
would. But I think that any child who
is old enough to read this little book is
old enough to need the Saviour and love
him too. You love your father, I suppose? Of course you do, for he loves
you, and takes very tender care of you.
But Jesus loves you much better than
your father, and watches over you far
more tenderly. *He* loves you well enough
to die for you. And can't you love him
just as you do your own father? If you
can't, you must be a very hard-hearted
little child. But I think you can. At
any rate, I want to help you to try; for
I don't believe Jesus would have " died
for *all* " unless he felt that all, even the
youngest, needed him, and wanted all to

love him. Your little baby brother can't
know anything about Jesus yet, and of
course he can't love him. But if you
are old enough to have your kind mother
or sister tell you about Jesus, you are
quite old enough to love him, and he
longs to have you do so.

You remember, when Jesus was on
earth, that one day, in the wild, rough
country over beyond the river Jordan,
the people brought little children to the
Saviour, "that he might put his hands
on them and pray." Jesus' friends were
very much annoyed at this, and tried to
stop it. Perhaps they thought that their
Master was tired, for he had been talking a great deal that day. Perhaps
they thought, as some do now, that
Jesus could not do such little children

any good. But Jesus did not think so. Indeed, he was grieved with his friends for sending the people away. He loved the little children, and called them to himself. He took them up in his arms, put his hands upon them, and blessed them. It must have been a touching sight to see the little children nestling up to the bosom of the Great Teacher, won by his gentle smile and kind words. I am sure you would have loved him if you could have seen him *then;* and he is just the same gentle and loving Saviour now.

When Jesus called the little children to himself, he said, "SUFFER LITTLE CHIL-DREN TO COME UNTO ME, AND FORBID THEM NOT, FOR OF SUCH IS THE KINGDOM OF HEAVEN." You may learn these precious words, and repeat them in the Sabbath-school concert, and when you say them think — Jesus meant that for *me;* he wants *me* to come to him. There will be many little children in heaven besides the dear one of whom you have been reading. I have two little sisters and a little brother who died before they were old enough to know much about Jesus; but I have no doubt that they are in Jesus' arms now, and know much more about him than we do. And I think there are a great many more little children there, who came from China and Burmah and the islands of the sea to Jesus' bosom, — so many, indeed, that Jesus could truthfully call heaven " the little children's heaven;" for that is what he means when he says, " Theirs is the

kingdom of heaven." You remember
the little hymn which begins —

"Little travellers Zionward,
Each one entering into rest,
In the kingdom of your Lord,
In the mansions of the blest"? —

It is a very beautiful and true hymn,
but sometimes it makes me sad when I
hear it sung, for I think that there will
be many more little children than grown
persons in heaven, and I want *all* to go
there.

If you had died when you were a little
baby, I am very sure that Jesus would
have taken you right to heaven, and
taught you there to love himself. But
even then he would have had to give you
a new heart; for Jesus himself tells us

that "that which is born of the flesh is flesh, and that which is born of the Spirit is spirit," — a verse which means that no one, not even the youngest child, can love Jesus unless God's blessed Spirit helps him. Jesus did not forget this when the little children clustered about him; but he meant to help the very youngest of them to love him, and he knew that even the older ones were so innocent and trustful that it would be much easier for *them* to give their hearts to him than for grown persons who had long been sinning against him. He meant to *make* it easier for them, and he will make it easier for you now than it will be by and by, when you have become men and women.

As I was telling you, if you had died before you were old enough to know anything about Jesus, he would have given you a new and loving heart, and taken you right to himself. But now you are old enough to know him, and love him, and choose for yourself whether you will go to heaven or not. And Jesus means to let you choose for yourself, for he don't want to force anybody to go to heaven against their will. He sees that you are a sinner, and that you would n't be happy in such a holy place as heaven is unless your little heart was changed. I do not mean that you have done *very* wicked things; but, unless you are different from many little girls and boys whom I have seen, you may have been vexed with your kind parents

and playmates, or told little fibs, or
taken little things which did not belong
to you, or used naughty words. All
these are sins, and it is a *great* sin to
know the blessed Jesus, and not love
him and serve him. If you have done
this, Jesus is very much grieved with
you.

Perhaps you feel that you are a sinner
sometimes. If you do, you must not be
discouraged. You must remember that
Jesus came into this world on purpose
to save sinners, and that he wants very
much to save you. You must feel that
you need him, and believe that he is
able and willing to save you. You
must go right to Jesus, and tell him
that you are a naughty little child, and
want him to help you love him and

serve him. If you are really in earnest, he will help you to do so, and then you will be fit for heaven, and long to go and be with Jesus in his beautiful and happy home. And when you come to die, the loving Saviour will take *you* up in his arms, and put his hands upon you and bless you, as he did the little children whom he met on earth.

Perhaps you may not understand all that I have written; but my precious sister, of whom I have told you, did understand it all, and realize it all, before she was thirteen years old. She died when she was just as old as Jesus was when he went up to Jerusalem with his parents, and asked the doctors such hard questions in the temple. I have thought that it might help some little

boy or girl to love this wonderful Jesus
if they knew how dearly little Mary
loved him, and what a precious Saviour
he was to her. Dear little girl! she is
with Jesus in heaven now; and I have
written this little book, which tells you
all about her, that you may go there
too.

THE END.

Valuable Works,

PUBLISHED BY

GOULD AND LINCOLN.

——∽∘⦂⦂∘○——

HUGH MILLER'S WORKS. 7 vols. Testimony of the Rocks, 1.25.
— Schools and Schoolmasters, 1.25. — Footprints of the Creator, 1.00.
— Old Red Sandstone, 1.25. — First Impressions of England, 1.00.
— Cruise of the Betsey, 1.25. — Popular Geology, 1.25.
The above sold separately, or in uniform style, with elegant box, 8.25.

CHAMBERS'S CYCLOPÆDIA OF ENGLISH LITERATURE.
With Illustrations. 2 vols. Cloth, 5.00 ; sheep extra, 6.00 ; cloth,
full gilt, 7.50.

CHAMBERS'S MISCELLANY. 10 vols. Cloth, 7.50 ; cloth, gilt,
10.00 ; library sheep, 10.00.

CHAMBERS'S HOME BOOK. 6 vols. Cloth, with box, 3.00.

CYCLOPÆDIA OF ANECDOTES. Arvine. Illustrations. Octavo, cloth. 3.00.

CYCLOPÆDIA OF BIBLICAL LITERATURE. Kitto. 3.00.

ANALYTICAL CONCORDANCE OF THE BIBLE. Eadie. 3.00.

DR. HARRIS'S WORKS. The Great Teacher, 85 cts. — The Great
Commission, 1.00.— Pre-Adamite Earth, 1.00.— Man-Primeval, 1.25.
— Patriarchy, 1.25. — Sermons on Special Occasions, 2 vols., 2.00.

VISITS TO EUROPEAN CELEBRITIES. Sprague. Cloth. 1.00.

THE GREYSON LETTERS. Henry Rogers. 12mo, cloth. 1.25.

KNOWLEDGE IS POWER. Knight. 12mo, cloth, 1.25.

LIFE OF MONTGOMERY. Mrs. Knight. 12mo, cloth. 1.25.

LIFE OF AMOS LAWRENCE. 12mo, cloth, 1.00 ; octavo, 1.50.

MY MOTHER. 12mo, cloth, 75 cents ; full gilt, 1.25.

THE EXCELLENT WOMAN. Sprague. 12mo, cloth. 1.00.

ESSAYS IN BIOGRAPHY AND CRITICISM. Peter Bayne.
2 vols., 12mo, cloth. Each 1.25.

THE CHRISTIAN LIFE. Peter Bayne. 12mo, cloth. 1.25.

THE BETTER LAND. Thompson. 12mo, cloth. 85 cents.

HEAVEN. Kimball. Cloth, 1.00 ; cloth, gilt, 1.50.   **(1)**

Valuable Religious Works,

PUBLISHED BY

GOULD AND LINCOLN.

LIMITS OF RELIGIOUS THOUGHT. Prof. H. Longueville Mansel. 12mo, cloth. 1.00.

THE HISTORICAL EVIDENCES OF THE TRUTH OF THE SCRIPTURE RECORDS. Rawlinson. 12mo, cloth. 1.25.

ILLUSTRATIONS OF SCRIPTURE; suggested by a visit to the Holy Land. Prof. Hackett. 1.00.

LESSONS AT THE CROSS; Rev. Samuel Hopkins. 16mo. 75c.

SALVATION BY CHRIST. Discussions on the leading Doctrines of the Bible. Dr. Wayland. 12mo, cloth. 1.00.

THE GREAT DAY OF ATONEMENT. Nebelin. 12mo, cl. 75.

EXTENT OF THE ATONEMENT. New edition. T. W. Jenkyn, D. D. 12mo, cloth. 1.00.

PHILOSOPHY OF THE PLAN OF SALVATION. Cloth. 75c.

YAHVEH CHRIST; or, The Memorial Name. MacWhorter. 60c.

THE MISSION OF THE COMFORTER. Julius Charles Hare. 12mo, cloth. 1.25.

CHRIST IN HISTORY. R. Turnbull, D. D. Cloth. 1.25.

LEADERS OF THE REFORMATION — Luther, Calvin, Latimer, Knox. By Dr. Tulloch. 12mo, cloth. 1.00.

THE GREAT CONCERN. N. Adams, D. D. Cloth. 85 cents.

EVENINGS WITH THE DOCTRINES. Dr. N. Adams. Soon.

THE EVIDENCES OF CHRISTIANITY. Bolton. Cloth. 80c.

THE RELIGIONS OF THE WORLD. Prof. Frederick Denison Maurice. Cloth. 60 cents.

CHRISTIAN WORLD UNMASKED. John Berridge. Cloth. 50c.

THE EVENING OF LIFE. J. Chaplin, D. D. Cloth. 1.00.

THE STATE OF THE IMPENITENT DEAD. Prof. Alvah Hovey, D. D. 50 cents.

BAXTER'S SAINT'S EVERLASTING REST. 16mo, cloth. 50 cents.   (2)

Valuable Religious Works,

PUBLISHED BY

GOULD AND LINCOLN.

————∞◦⸰❦⸰◦∞————

GOTTHOLD'S EMBLEMS; or, Invisible Things Understood by Things that are Made. Christian Scriver. 8vo, cloth, 1.00; fine edition, tinted, 1.50.

THE STILL HOUR; or, Communion with God. Prof. Austin Phelps, D. D. 16mo, cloth. 38 cents.

THE CRUCIBLE; or, Tests of a Regenerate State. Rev. J. A. Goodhue. Introduction by E. N. Kirk, D. D. 12mo, cloth. 1.00.

NEW ENGLAND THEOCRACY. From the German of Uhden. Introduction by Neander. H. C. Conant. 12mo, cloth. 1.00.

CHRISTIAN BROTHERHOOD. Baron Stow, D.D. Cloth. 50 cts.

FIRST THINGS; or, The Development of Church Life. Baron Stow, D. D. 16mo, cloth. 60 cents.

THE HARVEST AND THE REAPERS. Home Work for All, and How to do it. Rev. H. Newcomb. 16mo, cloth. 63 cents.

LECTURES ON THE LORD'S PRAYER. William R. Williams, D. D. 12mo, cloth. 85 cents.

RELIGIOUS PROGRESS; or, Development of Christian Character. W. R. Williams, D. D. 12mo, cloth. 85 cents.

CHRISTIAN PROGRESS. A Sequel to The Anxious Inquirer. John Angell James. 18mo, cloth. 31 cents.

CHRISTIAN'S DAILY TREASURY: Religious Exercises for every Day in the Year. Rev. E. Temple. 12mo, cloth. 1.00.

CHURCH MEMBER'S GUIDE. John Angell James. Edited by Dr. Choules. Introduction by Hubbard Winslow. Cloth. 33 cts.

THE CHURCH IN EARNEST. J. A. James. 18mo, cloth. 40 cts.

THE PREACHER AND THE KING; or, Bourdaloue in the Court of Louis XIV. From the French of L. F. Bungener. Introduction by Geo. Potts, D. D. 12mo, cloth. 1.25.

COMMENTARY ON THE ACTS OF THE APOSTLES. Prof. H. B. Hackett, D. D. Octavo, cloth. 2.25.

CRUDEN'S CONDENSED CONCORDANCE. Complete Concordance to the Holy Scriptures. Edited by David King, LL.D. Octavo, cloth backs, 1.25; sheep, 1.50.   **(3)**

Valuable Works,

PUBLISHED BY

GOULD AND LINCOLN.

——∘∘⦂⧉⦂∘∘——

THE PULPIT OF THE REVOLUTION; or, Sermons of the Era of 1776. Introduction, Biographical Sketches of the Preachers, Historical Notes, etc. J. Wingate Thornton. 12mo, cloth.

FOOTSTEPS OF OUR FOREFATHERS: What they Suffered and what they Sought. J. G. Miall. Illustrations. 12mo, cl. 1.00.

MEMORIALS OF EARLY CHRISTIANITY: Presenting, in a graphic, popular form, Memorable Events of Early Ecclesiastical History. J. G. Miall. Illustrations. 12mo, cloth. 1.00.

THE MISSIONARY ENTERPRISE ; Discourses on Christian Missions, by distinguished American Clergymen. Edited by Baron Stow, D. D. 12mo, cloth. 85 cents.

THE LIFE AND CORRESPONDENCE OF JOHN FOSTER. J. E. Ryland 12mo, cloth. 1.25.

MEMOIR OF THE LIFE AND TIMES OF ISAAC BACKUS. Prof. ALVAH HOVEY, D. D. 12mo, cloth. 1.25.

PHILIP DODDRIDGE. His Life and Labors. John Stoughton. D. D. 16mo, cloth. 60 cents.

KIND WORDS FOR CHILDREN, to Guide them in the Path of Peace. Rev. H. NEWCOMB. 16mo, cloth. 42 cents.

GATHERED LILIES; or, Little Children in Heaven. Rev. A. C. THOMPSON. 18mo, flexible cloth. 25 cents.

OUR LITTLE ONES IN HEAVEN. Edited by the Author of the "Aimwell Stories." 18mo, cloth. 50 cents.

APOLLOS; or, Directions to Persons just commencing a Religious Life. 32mo, paper covers, cheap, for distribution. 6 cents.

SAFE HOME; or, the Last Days of Fanny Kenyon. Introduction by Prof. J. L. LINCOLN. 18mo, flexible cloth. 25 cents.

PILGRIMAGE TO EGYPT; Manners, Customs, and Institutions of the People. Hon. J. V. C. Smith. Illustrations. 12mo, cl. 1.25.

THE CRUISE OF THE NORTH STAR. A Voyage to England, Russia, Denmark, France, Spain, Italy, Malta, Turkey, Madeira, &c. Rev. JOHN O. CHOULES, D. D. Elegant Illustrations. 12mo, cloth, gilt backs and sides. 1.50. **(4)**

Valuable Works,

PUBLISHED BY

GOULD AND LINCOLN.

————o◦ৡৡ◦o————

GOD REVEALED IN NATURE AND IN CHRIST. James B. Walker. 12mo, cloth. 1.00.

PERSON AND WORK OF CHRIST. Ernest Sartorius, D. D., Prussia. Tr. by Rev. O. S. Stearns. 18mo, cloth. 42 cents.

THE SUFFERING SAVIOUR. Krummacher 12mo, cloth. 1.25.

WREATH AROUND THE CROSS; or, Scripture Truths Illustrated. A. Morton Brown, D. D. 16mo, cloth. 60 cents.

THE SCHOOL OF CHRIST; or, Christianity Viewed in its Leading Aspects. A. L. R. Foote. 16mo, cloth. 50 cents.

THE IMITATION OF CHRIST. Thomas a Kempis. Life by Ullman. 12mo, cloth. 85 cents.

SERVICE, THE END OF LIVING. Rev. A. L. Stone, 16mo, flexible cloth. 20 cents.

MOTHERS OF THE WISE AND GOOD. Jabez Burns, D. D. 16mo, cloth. 75 cents.

THE PRIEST AND THE HUGUENOT; or, Persecution in the Age of Louis XV. From the French of L. F. Bungener. 2 vols. 12mo, cloth. 2.25.

MODERN ATHEISM. James Buchanan, LL.D. 12mo, cl. 1.25.

DR. TWEEDIE'S WORKS. — Glad Tidings, 16mo, cloth, 63 cts. — A Lamp to the Path, 63 cts. — Seed Time and Harvest, 63 cts.

THE HALLIG; or, The Sheepfold in the Waters. From the German of Biernatski. Mrs. Geo. P. Marsh. Cloth. 1.00.

THE SIGNET RING, and its Heavenly Motto. 16mo. 31 cents.

SOCIAL PRAYER MEETINGS. By late Bishop Alexander Viets Griswold, D. D. 12mo, cloth, flexible covers. 25 cents.

DR. GRANT AND THE MOUNTAIN NESTORIANS. Rev. T. Laurie. Portrait, Map, and Illustrations. 12mo, cl. 1.25.

THE HISTORY OF PALESTINE. John Kitto, D. D. Illustrations. 12mo, cloth. 1.25.　　　　　**(5)**